Text Game

by

Kate Cann

First published in 2004 in Great Britain by
Barrington Stoke Ltd
18 Walker St, Edinburgh EH3 7LP

www.barringtonstoke.co.uk

Reprinted 2004, 2005, 2006, 2007

ISBN: 978-1-84299-148-0

Printed in Great Britain by Bell & Bain Ltd

A Note from the Author

When you write for teenagers, you have to be aware how quickly things date.
I've learnt not to name celebrities or fashions or music in my books, because six months down the line they will be old news. I'm quite happy with that, because I think it means I focus on the real things that don't change – like love and anger and happiness and jealousy!

However, texting is different. That's new, but I think it's here to stay for a long while yet. It really has changed the way teenagers relate to each other. Texting means you can always be in touch with everyone, and that's not always good. I've thought a lot about the power of texting, the way it can be both good and bad.

This book is based on a true story, but I can't tell you what it is or I'll give the plot away!

To Aidan –
thanks for the brilliant idea for the
cover of this book!

Contents

Chapter 1
Too Good For Me

My friend Lisa's glaring at me. I've just told her I'm going to a party next Friday with Ben, my new boyfriend. And she's reminded me it's our old mate Ryan's birthday that day. And I'm thinking, *Sod it!*

"Look," she says, "look, Mel, you can't miss Ryan's birthday."

"Oh, come on," I squawk, "he hasn't arranged anything."

"Yeah, but he always leaves things till the last minute. You know he's gonna want to do something."

There's a pause. Then Lisa demands, "You gonna let Ryan down?"

"I don't know!" I huff.

"You can't! Honestly, Mel! Just tell Ben that Ryan's a really good mate of yours and it's his birthday. You're going *out* with Ben – you're not joined to him at the hip!"

I make a face at Lisa, because I know she's right. In the past we've both laughed at girls who do everything their boyfriend does. And I can't let Ryan down. It's just that I don't want to miss that party. I don't want to miss going there with Ben.

"It's not as though you've only just started going out with Ben," Lisa goes on smugly, because she knows she's right. "How long has he been around now?"

"Seven weeks and two days since we first went out. Eight weeks and five days since we first talked. Ten weeks—"

"Oh, *spare* me!" groans Lisa. "I know, I know – ten weeks, three days, eight minutes, twenty seconds since you first set eyes on him and turned into this sad blob of love and obsession! Can't you think of anything except Ben?"

I swipe at her, and we both laugh.

"I can't help it," I moan. "He's *so* gorgeous. Don't you think he's gorgeous?"

"He's OK. Nice body."

"*Nice?* It's fantastic. *He's* fantastic. And he's great with it – not at all up himself like most good-looking boys are. He's a laugh. He cracks me up. And he thinks about me too, about what I think. When we're talking he *listens* to me!"

"Well, *wow*! Phone the telly, get it on the six o'clock news!"

"Oh, shut up! I just can't get over how lucky I am, that's all. That Ben asked me out. That we're still together."

"Oh, Mel, he likes you too! Watch my lips – *he-likes-you-too.* Why is that so amazing? Of course he likes you! *You're* funny too and you're clever and great company and you know what? I think he's the lucky one! *He's* lucky to be going out with *you*!"

My eyes have gone all wet and blurry. Lisa and I don't go in for the kind of kissy-kissy, touchy-feely stuff that a lot of girls do, so when Lisa says something like this to me it's special. "Thanks," I croak.

"You're welcome. And I mean it, OK?"

"OK. It's just—"

"Just what?"

4

"It's just … he's too good for me, that's all. I know he is."

There's a silence. Lisa has got that look on her face, the look that says she's working something out and I'd better not interrupt. It's the look that says she's about to come out with something I might not like but she's going to come out with it anyway.

"For one," she says at last, "that's rubbish. Like I said, he's the lucky one. And two, you know what'll really screw things up, don't you?"

"What?"

"You being like this – *acting* like this. All grateful and keen, like you can't see what he sees in you, like you're not as good as him. I mean, maybe one day he'll start seeing you like that too."

My head droops. Again, she's right.

"Look, I'm not going to kid you," she goes on. "He's *great* looking. And you're sexy and gorgeous but out of you two he's the one more likely to get chosen to do a photo shoot, OK?"

"*Exactly.* When I'm out with him I see all these girls eyeing him, and—"

"And he's still out with you. He's *with* you. Mel, you've got to trust him! You think he's fantastic – tell yourself he's thinking the exact same about you! You're trying to please him too much, fit in with him too much. He asked you out because he likes you just the way you *are*. He doesn't want you to turn into this ... this *creep.* So come on. You tell him you can't make the party. And if *he* can't bear a night apart from you, ask him to come out with us to Ryan's."

Chapter 2
The Next Level

I see Ben later that day and the first thing I do is tell him about Ryan's birthday.

"So who *is* Ryan?" Ben demands. "And how come I've never met him if he's such a big friend that you can't miss his birthday?"

My first thought is how gorgeous Ben looks with his forehead all scrunched up and this sexy, cross little crease between his eyebrows. My second thought is, *My God, he's jealous. He really is jealous!*

This is almost too fabulous to deal with. I fight to stop my face splitting into a big smile and say, "Oh, Ryan and I have been friends since Year *Seven*. We started off going out together for about half a term ..."

"So he's an ex?" Ben asks.

"Ben, we were 11 years old. He hardly counts as an ex-boyfriend."

"But you've stayed friends."

"Yeah. He's great. I can be really open with him, tell him anything. Once you've practised snogging with someone when you're both 11, you do stay friends."

"Do you still fancy him?"

"*No!* God, I've watched him grow up. It'd be like incest, like going out with your brother."

"So he's like a brother then?"

"Wow! Razor-brain. Yeah."

Ben grins at the insult. "Hey, you. Watch it!"

"OK," I laugh. "Look, you're right – it's time you met him. Why don't you come out with us too?"

Ben's thinking hard. He's frowning. I'm full of wanting to kiss him to smooth the frown away. There's a pause, then he says, "I promised Joe I'd go to his party. It's a big deal for him, having this party. His parents are dead fussy. He wants me there in case there's trouble and stuff."

"Well, you've gotta go then," I say.

"And you've gotta be there for Ryan's birthday," Ben answers.

"Yep. We're gonna have to have a Friday night apart."

"How mature is that?" he says, leaning in very close to me.

"Very. Very mature."

"Mind-bloody-bogglingly mature."

I laugh, and reach out for his hand, and it closes round mine as if we're making a pact, proof he's feeling the same way I am. Full of wanting, full of liking. And then he leans in even closer and our mouths collide and we have the best kiss in the history of humankind.

And after that, for the few days before Friday night, it's like we've shifted up to the next level. Crossed over to somewhere new.

I feel stronger, more confident. I've *almost* got over being stunned Ben wants to go out with me. I've started to really trust him, trust he likes me. On this new level, everything feels fantastic and it's getting better all the time. We're talking more, touching more, opening up, as if we've said to each other, *Relax, just be you, it's you I want to be with.* It's the best.

Chapter 3
The Text

Some nights things feel like they're as good as they can get. I've got money in my purse, I've got a gorgeous new top on, and I'm out with all my mates for Ryan's birthday, starting off at the pizza place.

We're all warm and easy, saying how we don't see enough of each other now we're at college, talking about going clubbing next weekend. And we're ordering more drinks and the night's lifting off and I feel *great.*

"All right, Mel," says Ryan, turning to me, "how's the big romance going?"

"It's big," I grin. "It's going!"

Everyone laughs, groans. "Why didn't you bring him along tonight?" my friend Chloe demands.

"'Cos she knew you'd try and get hold of him, you slag!" caws Lisa.

"He had to go to some big party," I say.

"Aw, and weren't you invited?"

"I wanted to be with you lot! We're not joined at the hip!"

Lisa smiles across the table at me then pouts her lips all jokey and mouths, *proud of you, babe!*

Ryan puts his arm around me and crows, "So touched you chose to be here to celebrate the amazing fact of my birth, Mel! Cheers!"

The pizza arrives and everyone digs in. Lisa divides it up bossily and slaps at Greg's hand for trying to take two bits. I chew my first, big, juicy bite and think about Ben at his party, missing me like I'm missing him, and how great it's going to be seeing him tomorrow night. I think, *If we do all go to a club next weekend, I'll get him to come too. Then he can meet Ryan and get to know all my mates, like a real boyfriend.*

Chloe starts making everyone laugh by telling us about her posh cousin's wedding and, just as she's describing how much champagne she drank and how much cake icing she ate, I get a text. I pull my phone out, and Ryan says, "Oh, lord, a slurpy message from loverboy?" And, smiling, I read it.

`hey, dog-girlfriend - mayb u shuda cum 2 da party wid B!`

I carry on smiling but I feel like someone's put a knife in me. All the good feeling's drained away. I choke down a couple more mouthfuls of pizza then I stand up and go to the toilets.

Lisa follows me in. We've been friends so long she knows when I'm upset. Before she can ask, I shove my phone at her with the text still glowing.

"Christ," she mutters. "*Nice.*"

"That means he's got off with someone," I croak. "Doesn't it? At the party."

"*No.* It means some sicko wants you to *think* that."

"Who is it? Who'd do it?"

"Phone 'em back. Go on."

"They know me. They know about me and Ben."

"Go *on*, Mel! Now!"

I punch in the number, all shaky. It rings three times then there's party background noise and a girl going, "Yeah, *yeah?*"

"You texted me. You—"

"Oh damn," the girl gurgles, then her voice goes away from the phone and she shrieks, "*Glo*, you idiot—" And the phone goes dead.

I tell Lisa what happened.

"Glow?" she says. "What did she tell you to *glow* for?"

"I dunno."

"Phone her back again. Go on."

"I *can't.* God, I feel sick."

"Phone Ben then."

"What, and make him think I'm checking up on him?"

There's a silence. Lisa puts her arm around me and we stay there by the sinks and she tries to comfort me and persuade me the text doesn't mean a thing.

"She could've got your number from anyone – she's just a sad little psycho, someone with sick ideas, trying to stir it, 'cos she's jealous about Ben ..."

"Yeah. And she's at the party with Ben."

"Yeah, OK, but it doesn't mean she's *with* him, does it? Come on – she's *mad*, sending that, telling you to glow! Why would he want to be with a complete loony, eh?"

I manage a smile and Lisa squeezes my shoulders and says, "If we stay in here much longer, someone'll come looking for us. Look, tomorrow morning, soon as you've got up, phone Ben, tell him about the text and ask him who it could be. Tonight – try and forget about it, yeah?"

I agree, and we go back to the table.

But the text is working in my brain like a maggot.

Chapter 4

The Maggot

Ever since I started going out with Ben, I've felt great when I wake up in the morning, kind of happy, excited. But when I get up this morning there's something horrible turning and twisting in my mind, spoiling everything, and I know it's that text.

I crawl down to the kitchen, glad to find it empty of family, make myself tea and toast and try to work out what to do. I know I should phone Ben, like Lisa said, and tell him about the text. Or ask to meet him this morning, and show the text to him.

17

Because I've saved it. I went to delete it on my phone, and then at the last minute, I didn't. I don't understand why.

I pour my second mug of tea. I really don't want to tell Ben about the text. I tell myself it's because I don't want to make a fuss – make the stupid message more important than it is. But that's not the real reason. It's because I can't face doing it. In case something in Ben's voice or on his face tells me I'm right to worry like this.

Sod it, sod it. It's like my mind and emotions are in a washing machine, going round and round, all jumbled up, getting nowhere.

The house phone goes. I want it to be Ben, but I'm scared to talk to him. I pick it up and say hello and Lisa chirps, "Hi, Mel! Have you phoned Ben yet?"

I feel this rush of anger at her. "Christ, give me a chance," I snap. "I've only just woken up!"

"Sorry," she mutters. "Just – I gotta go out, and I was wondering ..."

"You were the one saying that text meant nothing."

"Yeah, but—"

"I'll ask him when I see him, OK?"

"OK. Well ... see you later then."

"Yeah. See you."

Funny how talking can run on two tracks at once. The words we're using as we say goodbye are fine, but this big, cold space has suddenly opened up between us. She's upset because she thinks I've snapped at her, and I feel ... *God*, I feel angry with her. Why doesn't she just keep out of it? I don't trust her advice any more for a start. If I hadn't followed her advice about choosing Ryan's birthday over Joe's party, this whole maggoty mess wouldn't have happened, would it? She's to blame for that maggot eating at my mind.

I have quite a busy Saturday, even though I've got nothing planned. I wash my new top so I can wear it again tonight when I meet Ben. I finish off an essay. Then Mum nags at me to walk the dog so I change into my tracksuit and go running with him because I'm trying to get fit. I even do 30 sit-ups afterwards. Then I sort out my room a bit and watch some TV.

That's what I'm doing on the surface. Underneath, I'm waiting to get another text from the psycho. The day feels like a tunnel, everything in it, everything in *me*, focused on meeting Ben at eight o'clock. I'm dreading getting another text before I get there.

I leave my phone in my bag on the hall table. I check it at midday to find a missed call from Ryan, and a text. I feel sick till I see that the text's from Chloe –

`at Costa Coffee – cum down`

I don't call back – well, I'm busy, aren't I?

At three I check my phone again. This time, there are two texts waiting. One from Lisa –

`r u OK? Call me!`

Why can't she leave me alone?

Then there's a lovely one from Ben –

`How was last nyt? Want 2 c u now not 2nyt!`

This makes me think everything's all right, until it hits my brain that he could just be being so sweet because he's feeling guilty.

I text him back –

`fine, c u soon`

– because I can't think of anything more to say.

At half past six I make myself check my phone one more time. Nothing. I feel a wave of relief and race upstairs quickly. I tell myself that last night's text was a one-off, just a sick, drunk trick. I tell myself that this time tomorrow I'll have forgotten all about it.

Then I lock myself in the bathroom and start getting ready to go out.

Chapter 5

Glo

I love getting ready to go out, all the ritual of creaming and cleaning and grooming and pampering. By the time I'm out of the shower and putting on my make-up, slowly and carefully, enjoying the way my face is transformed, I feel really good.

I go through to my bedroom, paint my nails, wave them till they're dry and pull my clothes on (my top's still a bit damp, but it doesn't matter, it looks great). Then I set off to meet Ben at the pub. I'm really excited.

It only takes me 15 minutes to walk there. It's called The Dog and Duck, and it's scruffy and run-down, but the landlord isn't too fussy about your age so it tends to be full of kids. It's loud and fun. A good place to meet.

Ben's got there before me, but I see him before he sees me. He's sprawling on the bench in the corner, all long-legged and gorgeous, and the sudden thought hits my brain that he could have pulled someone else last night and I want to *scream.*

He looks up and sees me and it's like his face shifts into focus. I bite back the scream. He breaks into his wonderful, sexy grin and scrambles to his feet.

"You look great, Mel!"

"It's a new top. Like it?"

"Yeah. But that's not why you look great."

He pulls me down beside him on the bench. He's already got me a drink. I almost can't look at him but it's just so good being close to him. I can smell the stuff he puts on his hair, hear him breathing. I want to creep inside his open jacket, press myself against his chest, beg him to tell me nothing happened last night.

Instead I snatch up my drink and say, "So was it fun? Your party?"

"Nah, not really. Boring."

"Yeah? Who was there?"

"Oh, the usual lot. And Joe's cousins. Real geeks, the lot of 'em."

"Well, why was it boring, if it was with all your friends?"

He glances at me, like he thinks I'm being weird, and says, "*You* weren't there."

I still can't look at him. He slides his hand up the back of my neck, turns my face towards him and kisses me.

That's another good thing about The Dog and Duck. The landlord's not fussy about what he calls "petting", as long as it's not too open. We have a long, long kiss, and I wrap myself into him, and I feel so good. He likes me, he wants me. Nothing happened last night, I know it.

So prove it, says a voice in my head. *Show him the text.*

I won't listen to the voice. I can't bear to spoil things, spoil the way he's got his arm around me.

He asks me about Ryan's birthday, and I tell him what we did, and he tells me about a motorbike he went to look at today, and talks about how much he wants to get one, and we kiss again.

And the evening goes on, and we're chatting and laughing and flirting, and I tell myself nothing's changed, it's as good as ever.

Apart from the maggot wriggling and niggling round the edges of my brain.

We get into a moan about college and how boring and dull most of the people there are and then, out of the blue, he draws back from me and says, "What's up, Mel?"

"How d'you mean?"

"I dunno. You're all ... tense. On edge. Has something happened?"

My heart thumps. *Tell him, tell him,* says the voice.

"Do I? Oh, I'm just knackered. I've had it."

"Yeah? Well you were out too late last night, weren't you, you piss 'ead!"

"Shut up!" I dig my fingers into his leg, and he puts his arm back around me and crunches my shoulders up till I squeal at him to stop. Then we have another kiss, slow and really great. And, just as our mouths are sliding away from each other, I get a text.

I feel sick with panic at the sound. I should've turned my phone off. Left it at home. Smashed it up.

"Aren't you gonna read it?" says Ben, rubbing his cheek against my hair.

"It'll keep," I mutter.

It keeps. The message stays in my phone until I get to the pub toilets, three minutes later. My hands shake as I pull my phone from my bag, praying it's Chloe, praying it's Lisa.

But it isn't. And this time it's from a new number.

ask B bout last nyt, look in da mirror, wen it crak, put 2 + 2 2gether

It's like a 21st century witch's spell, like a curse. Like someone evil whispering at you in the dark and you can't see where they are.

Why two numbers? Two people? Two phones? I'm too shaky to phone this new number. I go back to Ben. I've got to tell him now, I've got to.

"So was last night good?" I ask. I'm doing just what the text told me to do. My voice comes out like a yap but he doesn't seem to notice.

He frowns. "Mel, I told you! You should'a been there!"

"Should I?"

"Well – maybe not. You'd've probably hated it. Too many people outta their heads … Glo had this bottle of vodka …"

The maggot writhes. "*Glow?*"

"Gloria. Girl I know."

"How well d'you know her?"

And he looks at the floor and waits too long before shrugging and saying, "Oh, not well."

So Glow's a girl. Glo. Short for Gloria. For the rest of that night it's like I'm frozen, my mind's somewhere else. When we talk, when we kiss, I'm not there, I'm separate. That voice in my head is telling me to ask him about the texts, but I can't. I'm so scared. Scared he'll lie, scared of the truth.

I knew it was too good to be true, me and Ben.

We both act out parts for the rest of the evening. No-one would guess we weren't just a normal couple, happy to be with each other. I act like nothing's wrong, like I'm just tired, and he acts – I don't want to think about what part he acts.

We say goodbye and hug and kiss like we always do and he says he'll phone and maybe we can see a film tomorrow.

****

I race home. I let myself in and run up to my room and lock the door. Then I text the number of the second message.

who is Glo?

Straight away, like she's been waiting for me, the answer comes back.

hi, dog. G = B's best luva

I sit there in the half-dark on my bed and things slot into place like bullets into a gun.

At the party Glo got hold of Ben's phone, found my number. 'Cos he'd taken his jacket off. With the rest of his clothes maybe. And

31

now she and her friend – the girl who
answered the phone that first time – they're
telling me about it.

Chapter 6

B's gonna dump u

I spend Sunday morning kind of locked in on myself, as if I'm holding my breath, waiting for something to happen. Ben phones around midday. "Hey," he says, "fancy getting out into the sunshine?"

I look towards the window. I didn't even know the sun was out, blazing down on the grey walls and pavements.

"I ... I can't," I say, before I can think. Two days ago, I'd've been out of the door and on my way to him. But now ...

"We've got people coming for lunch," I lie, "and I've got all this work to do ..."

"OK, OK," he says, "just one excuse'll do. Tonight then, yeah?"

We agree to meet at 7.30 under the town clock in the square and ring off. I set my phone on silent and flop down on my bed and cry because of the way everything's been turned inside out. I want to sleep. I want to lose myself in deep, dead sleep. But just as I'm drifting off, my phone vibrates. It's lying next to my hand and I feel it vibrate through my skin, right down to my bones, full of hate.

I know who it's going to be. It's the first number again.

B's gonna dump you, dog-face.

I lie there, heart thumping. There's some horrible pattern to this. Something horrible about the way this text arrived just half an hour after I told Ben I couldn't meet him.

Did he go and see Glo instead?

Did he go and see her because I wouldn't meet him?

Lisa phones me as I'm getting ready to meet Ben that evening. "Hey, where have you been?" she says. "I've been trying to get hold of you."

"Oh, sorry, just busy, you know ..."

"I was worried about you. Look, have you sorted things out with Ben? About that stupid text?"

I leave a pause, like I'm not even sure what she's on about, then I say, "Oh – the *text.* They were drunk and messing about. Someone got hold of his phone, that's all."

"Told you. Did he know who it was? Did he slap 'em?"

"It was just a *joke—*"

"Some joke. You were really upset."

"Yeah, well, I was stupid, OK?"

"OK, OK! I was only thinking of you!"

"Yeah, sorry. Look, Lisa, I gotta go – I'll phone you later, OK?"

And I hang up.

Inside the cinema I hold Ben's hand tight with one hand while the other rests on my phone in my pocket. Halfway through the film my phone starts to vibrate, like a beetle whirring in a matchbox. Quietly, I take it out. It's from the second number this time.

`B's playin wiv u`

I have this overwhelming feeling Glo's sitting somewhere behind us, spying on us, a witch in the dark, mocking me, cursing me. I slip my phone back in my pocket, and Ben, who's really into the film now, gives my hand a squeeze. He hasn't even noticed.

A week goes by, and I carry on seeing Ben, like nothing's happened, and I get sometimes

two, sometimes three texts a day. From both
numbers, but mostly the second.

    B told me how crap u r

    B + G = hot!

    B's gonna ditch u

Some of them know where we are, what
we're doing, like she's watching us.

    nice meal, bitch?

    u look shite 2nyt

    wow - boring pub again?

How can she *know* all this? She can't be
watching us, not all the time.

And then I realize. Of course. She knows
because Ben's telling her.

I feel ill the whole time, knotted up.
I can't eat, I sleep too much. For a few
moments, when I wake up, I feel OK, and then
I remember and feel bad again.

37

I make excuses not to see Lisa, or the others. I hardly ever return calls. It's like I'm frozen, waiting.

Ben keeps asking me what's wrong, why I've gone weird on him, but I don't tell him. It's gone way, way beyond showing him the texts. If I showed him, he'd deny everything, he'd wriggle out of it somehow. I make excuses, like I've had a fight with my mum, or I've got too much to do at college. He sounds so frustrated and mad with me sometimes I think he's going to finish with me, just like one text said –

B's gonna dump you, dog-face!

– but he doesn't.

I'm saving the texts, storing them, every twisted last one of them. I'm waiting for proof.

Then – at last – I get it.

Chapter 7

Crisis

It's Saturday afternoon and we're at his place, sitting in the living room with the TV on. We're not really watching it. His parents are out, and there's this tension in the air because we could go up to his room and get on his bed together, not to go all the way, just to get close, like we'd started to before all this happened.

I know he wants to suggest it but he doesn't know how to, not with the scratchy mood I've been in for the last couple of weeks. I pick up the remote and flick aimlessly through the channels, not really looking at any of them. Then I chuck the remote down on the coffee table again. It's lying right beside his mobile. "Why don't you get us a drink?" I say.

"OK," he goes. "What – Coke?"

"I really fancy a cuppa tea," I ask, knowing it'll take him longer to get that for me.

While he's gone I pick up his mobile and flick to the phone book. There she is. *Glo.* There's the number. The second number. And he said he hardly knew her. Why would you have the number of someone you hardly knew? I flick to his recent messages. There's one from me, one from someone about football practice, one from ...

The second number. Glo's number.

hope u gonna b dere 2nyt, luva!

I throw the phone back down.

Ben comes back into the room, holding two mugs of tea. I can't bear to look at him. I don't know what to do. I don't know if I'm ready to have it out with him yet, if I'm ready for us to finish yet. He sits down beside me and puts the tea down on the table. "What're you doing tonight?" I ask.

"Dunno," he says. "What d'you fancy doing?"

"Not much. I'm tired."

"Mel, you're always tired!"

"Well, there's nothing on, is there? There's nothing good to do, there never is."

"Tom's got a free house," he says. "He's gonna have people round."

"Wow," I say.

"*God*, Mel, what's wrong with you? You never used to be like this."

"Like what?"

"All ... touchy about everything."

"I'm not. Who's gonna be there?"

"Oh, you know, Chris and Joe. *Me.*"

"Which girls?"

"Well, Vix and Mandy, and Em, and—"

"Glo? Will *Glo* be there?"

He looks at me really strangely. "What you wanna know about *her* for?"

It's true, it has to be. He looks guilty as sin. I know he's hiding something. He's lying. I jump to my feet. "I don't want to go to some poxy party where it's just *your* friends, OK?" I scream. "You go if you want to!"

Then I stand up and storm out of his house, and he doesn't come after me.

And the next morning – of *course* – a new text is waiting for me.

    B + G all last nyt!

Chapter 8

Proof

It's over. I can't stand any more of this, it's like millions of maggots in my brain. It's *over*.

I phone Ben and tell him I've got to see him. I don't say sorry for screaming at him. He's dead distant with me, but he agrees to meet at Coffee Republic in an hour's time.

He's there before me, waiting for me, but he hasn't got me a coffee. I buy a café latte and carry it with shaking hands over to the table he's sitting at.

"OK, Mel," he says, and his face is grim, and his hands are moving on the tabletop like he's nervous. "What's this about, eh?"

"Here," I say, handing him my phone. "Read these."

He looks at me, looking for an answer in my frozen face, then he starts scrolling through the messages.

"What the *hell*?" he mutters. He goes kind of white. He glances up at me like he doesn't know me. Then he scrolls some more.

"I don't understand," he spits out. "The first one was two *weeks* ago. Why didn't you tell me about this before?" He finishes reading the texts. There's a long silence.

"You believed them, didn't you?" he says at last. "You believed this crap. You thought I had something going on with Glo."

"Well, you have, haven't you?" I croak. "You're seeing her."

God, the relief of saying it. Of saying it at *last.*

"*No*! Jesus, Mel – you think I'd—"

"How come she got my number?"

"I dunno! She stole my phone off me – at that party the other week—"

"So you're pretty *close,* then, aren't you? Closer than you said you were. Close enough for you to have her number in your phone, get *texts* from her—"

"You checked my phone!"

"*Yes*, I checked your phone! And I found her number!"

"*Mel,* I've known her since we were kids. She's just kind of ... around. In the group."

"She called you lover."

"Oh, for God's sake. She flirts sometimes. She's embarrassing."

"*Yeah*? She knows everything we're doing, where we *are*—"

"She must've followed us. Or asked about us. *Christ*, I can't believe you let her get away with this. Look, Glo's *sick*. She's done this before. Not with texts, but I know a couple she screwed up by spreading stories, *rumours.* The bloke believed them, and it broke them up."

"That's too *neat.* Way too neat. Why be friends with her if she's like that?"

"I told you, we all go way back! And I feel—"

"What?"

"I *used* to feel sorry for her. I didn't think she'd do it again."

Something snaps inside. I know what's been going on these last two weeks. And I'm going to rip the truth out of him if it kills me.

"You're *lying*! You *have* been seeing her, haven't you? All the time you've been with me, you've been with *her* too, haven't you? And she's been texting me – 'cos she wants you for herself! She wants me to back off! That's right, isn't it? *Isn't it?*"

The people on the table next to us are all turning around, staring. Ben's looking at me in disgust. "I've never touched her," he says. "Not once."

"I don't believe you!"

"*Fine.* I'm gonna phone her, get her here now, make her tell you, make her admit what she's done."

"*Right.* Go on. Phone her."

He pulls his phone out of his pocket, glaring at me. "She'll be pissing herself over this," he snarls. "I bet she can't believe her luck that she got away with it this long. That you *let* her get away with it this long."

47

"*Fine.* When she gets here, we'll know, won't we?"

There's a long, long, heart-thudding pause, and then suddenly he shoves his chair back hard from the table and turns on me like he wants to hit me.

"So you're gonna take the word of this *psycho*, but you won't believe me?" he snarls. "Mel, I thought we were close – I thought we had something good together! This – it's *sick*. You believe that *crap* in the texts, and not what's right there in front of you! Why didn't you tell me about them, back when they started? I can't *believe* what's been going on in your head! What you've been thinking – what you've been *doing*! All this time! You're the one who's been lying, not me! If you'd *told* me, at the start, I could've sorted it, I could've proved to you – I could've stopped it before, before—"

He breaks off, and looks straight at me, and it's like something dies and falls away in my brain, and I can see in his face that he's never lied to me, not once, and I can see that I've lost him.

I've lost Ben.

Chapter 9

Hiding

Ben doesn't phone Glo. There's no need. We both know it's over. He can't stand how I've acted, what I've turned into.

I make myself stand up and walk out of the café first, because I can't bear the thought of having to watch him walk away from me.

The next few days are the worst days ever.

I tell Mum I'm ill and I don't go into college. There's only the slightest chance I'd bump into Ben there because his timetable is so different to mine and anyway the college is such a huge place, but even that slightest chance is more than I want to risk.

Most of the time I stay in my room. I turn off my mobile and throw it right at the back of my wardrobe. I feel like I'll never use it again.

Lisa phones the house two nights running but I tell Mum I feel dreadful and I'll phone her back later.

I don't though.

Ben doesn't phone me. I try to tell myself there's no way I'm hoping he will but I know deep down I am. Hoping.

On Wednesday night Mum comes into my room with a cup of tea and sits down on the end of my bed and says, "OK, darling, this has gone on long enough. What's up?"

"I'm ill, I told you, I've got a bug, a virus ..."

"Virus my arse."

I look up, shocked. Mum never swears, not usually. "What is it, Melissa? Come on now. Tell me."

"I ... I ..."

I'm wondering how to get her off my back when I hear the doorbell go down in the hall.

Mum waits impatiently for my little brother to answer it. He's downstairs on the computer. But there's no sound of him getting up and in the end my mum mutters, "He's got his headphones on again," and stamps out of my bedroom, shutting the door with a bang.

A few minutes later my door opens again, but this time it's Lisa who comes in.

"Hi, you," she says.

And I burst into great, gasping, throat-tearing tears.

Chapter 10
Lisa Talks Straight

It doesn't take long for me to tell Lisa the whole story. When I get to the bit where I walk out of Coffee Republic, leaving Ben behind, I burst into tears again.

Lisa makes a move towards me but I'm too ashamed to let her comfort me. I scramble off the bed and get my phone out from the back of the wardrobe, then I hand it to her.

She scrolls through Glo's messages, swearing under her breath, and says, "I can't

believe you didn't tell me what was going on!
I thought we were best mates!"

"I know," I sniff. "I just ... I didn't want to
tell anyone. I didn't want to talk about it.
I thought the texts might just go away.
I dunno."

Lisa shakes her head, scrolls some more.
Finally, she throws the phone down on the
bed and says, "What a sad cow."

"Me, you mean."

"No, not *you.* Her."

"She's not sad – she's *evil.* I'd like to kill
her. I'd like to smash her lying face in. She
ruined the best thing that ever happened to
me."

Lisa's looking steadily at me with that
look she does, the one that means *you're not
going to like what I say but I'm going to say it
anyway.*

"*You* did that, Mel," she murmurs. "You ruined it. She might be sick, but the only power she had was the power you gave her."

I feel like Lisa's hit me over the head with a brick.

"God," I whimper, "why d'you have to be so hard on me?"

"'Cos I'm your best mate," she says, and then she leans forward and puts her arms around my neck, and this time I let her, I let her hug me.

"If you'd only *told* me," she says, "or told him, back at the start ..."

"I know, I know!" I wail. "I'm a stupid, jealous idiot. I should've trusted him more. I don't *deserve* him. I don't deserve a friend like you, either, I'm so *stupid* ..."

"Mel, shut up! Or I really am going to have to slap you."

"It's true!"

"No it's not. You were just … scared, that's all. Scared you weren't good enough, that he didn't really like you. And that sick cow used all that. But, look, you can put it right."

"Yeah?" I croak, wiping my eyes. "How?"

"Phone him up. Say sorry. Ask him to give you a second chance."

"Oh, no. Oh, I *couldn't.*"

"Why not?"

"Because … I haven't got the guts. I'm too ashamed. He'd only say no, anyway."

"He might not. He might say yes."

"But if he said no I couldn't bear it."

"So you'd sooner do nothing – never see him again – than take the risk he might say no? That's *really* logical, Mel."

"I know. It's stupid. But I can't phone him. No way. Never."

There's a tap at the door, and Mum comes in with a big, relieved smile and a tray with two mugs and a packet of biscuits on it.

"So, have you helped sort out love's young nightmare, Lisa?" she asks.

Lisa makes a face back at her, and I think, *Maybe I can go on living, after all.*

Maybe, years and years into the future, I'll get over this, and start to feel normal again.

Chapter 11
Depression

I go back to college the next day.

I've decided I'm going to focus on my work now. I feel like I've slammed a door shut on the lovely space inside me where I feel emotions and get excited and look forward to things, and I've crept into this dark, cramped little corner, where I might exist rather than live but at least I'll be safe for a while.

In my lessons I listen to every word my teachers say, fixing my eyes on their faces.

At lunchtime I hide away in the library and start researching an essay I've got to do.

I've got quite good at making myself stop thinking about Ben. If his face, or the feel of his arms around me, or his cottony, sexy smell rise up in me, I blank the thoughts out. I slam the door shut on them.

That night at home I have a big sort out of my room, clearing loads of rubbish and old books off my shelves, and laying out my college books, all in order.

I look up and Mum's standing in the doorway with a mug of cocoa for me. She smiles and nods.

"You want to do the same for your clothes," she says. "You can hardly fit another thing into your wardrobe."

"Yeah, well," I shrug. "When I've got time."

"Tell you what, give me a big bag of stuff for the charity shop, and I'll take you shopping this weekend. Treat you to something new – something you really like."

I make myself smile. It feels like wet string on my face.

"Thanks, Mum," I say. I know she's trying to be kind, to get me back into the flow of things, but it's hopeless. It's way too soon. She watches me for another few moments, then she goes out, shutting the door softly behind her.

Lisa and Chloe find me on Friday lunchtime at college and tell me it's all fixed up for us to go clubbing the next night.

"It'll be great," says Chloe happily. "There's a whole gang of us. We can meet up at Jane's first, and share a cab back ..."

"Ryan's up for it," adds Lisa. "And Pete, and Frazer ..."

"I'm not sure I'm coming," I mutter.

"Come on," says Lisa. "You gotta get your life back one day!"

"Yeah, but not yet. For one thing, I'd ruin it for you. Being a misery."

"We don't mind," says Chloe.

"Nah," agrees Lisa. "And if you're too much of a misery, we'll just buy you a couple of drinks!"

I look up at them, at their kind faces fixed on mine. They look so worried for me I want to cry.

"Can we make it next weekend, yeah?" I say. "Just gimme a bit of time, OK?"

Next Tuesday, at college, I see Ben in the distance. I'd know his shape and his hair and his walk anywhere. Just this glimpse of him makes my blood thud round my body in panic, in love, in grief, everything. I hurry away to hide.

Lisa corners me at the end of the day and has another go at me for not phoning Ben and saying I'm sorry. I snap at her to leave me alone, and she stomps off, offended.

And after that, I sort of start trying to avoid her. I know she means well – like I know she was right when she said the only power Glo had was the power I gave her – but I can't deal with it. Not now.

My phone goes very silent. No texts, no calls. Strange how quickly that can happen when you don't reply to people.

On Sunday night Mum has another of her little chats with me, on the general subject of all work and no play making Mel a dull girl. She asks me why I'm not off out anywhere and then asks gentle questions about my friends and who I see at college and it slowly dawns on me that she's really worried about me being really depressed.

When she's gone I sit on my bed and stare at the wall and think, *Maybe I am really depressed.*

And suddenly trying to block out Ben with college work seems stupid, insane, and I feel like I can't move, I can't do anything.

I don't go into college the next day.

Everyone leaves the house as usual in the morning and they think I'm leaving too but when they've gone I go back to bed with all my clothes on and pull the covers over my head.

I skip lunch. I keep dozing, waking, dozing again. As if I'd like to block out my life with sleep.

Then at three that afternoon I'm woken by the noise of a text.

It still makes my stomach clench up, that noise, even though Glo's messages stopped dead the day Ben and I split up. I pick up my phone and see there's a text from Lisa.

```
got 2 c u.   URGENT!!   Costa
Coffee 5 pm.   L xx
```

My heart starts thumping in fear. What's up? What's happened? Panicking, I phone her mobile but I just get her voice-mail.
I phone Chloe to see if she knows anything but there's no reply.

I sit on the edge of the bed and I know I've got to go to Costa Coffee. It's the last thing I want to do, leave this bed, leave the house, walk into a café full of people, but if Lisa's in trouble and wants to see me I can't let her down.

I've got to be there for her, haven't I?

My hands are shaking as I push open the heavy glass door to Costa Coffee. I look over

all the people, trying to find Lisa's face,
looking for her blue-black hair, but I can't see
her anywhere.

And then ...

Then I see Ben.

Chapter 12
The Beautiful Trick

We stare at each other, him sitting at a table, me standing in the door, and I think I'm going to turn and run out, but I don't. I take a couple of wobbly steps towards him and he stands up and mutters, "If you wanted to see me, you could've just asked. You didn't need to set this up."

"Set what up?" I ask. He hates me. His whole face hates me.

"Getting Lisa to text me ..."

"*Lisa?* She sent *me* a text. I came here to meet her ..."

He flicks his phone and chucks it down on the table between us. I take out my phone, pull up Lisa's message and chuck it down beside his phone.

His message says:

got 2 c u bout Mel. URGENT!! Costa Coffee 5 pm. Lisa

And mine says:

got 2 c u. URGENT!! Costa Coffee 5 pm. L xx

"She had no right to do that," I choke. "She was on at me to phone you, and say sorry ... and ..."

"And you wouldn't."

"It wasn't that. I didn't think you'd listen. After what I'd done."

70

There's a long, long pause. It seeps into my mind that he's come here to meet Lisa to talk about me. He could've just avoided anything to do with me like the plague.

"Can I get you a drink?" he asks gruffly, his voice low.

"I'll get it," I say, and scuttle over to the counter. That way, if he changes his mind, if he wants to go, he can leave me now, now while my back's turned and I can't see ...

He's still sitting there when I get back to the table with my steaming mug in my hand. I feel like I'm at the start of a very long walk along a very high tightrope.

But I'm going to do it. I'm not going to bottle out this time. Even if I come crashing down.

"I *wanted* to say sorry," I mutter, sitting opposite him. "I really did. I just thought you'd tell me to sod off if I did."

"I don't understand what happened, Mel. Why you kept quiet about those filthy texts. And why you just walked *out* on me."

Slowly, clumsily, I start to explain.

And we begin to talk – all through another cup of coffee, and another one after that.

We talk about how awful those two weeks were, neither of us knowing what was going on. We talk about me walking away from him because I was ashamed. He tells me how he went straight round to Glo's house and confronted her and told her she'd better not come near him again. He tells me how angry he felt with me for not trusting him. Too angry to phone.

Then he says, "I still don't understand why you were taken in like that."

And I take in a big breath and mutter, "Because I was expecting something like that to happen. Because I couldn't believe you really wanted to go out with me."

There's a long silence, then he mutters back, "I felt the same way. I thought you were going off me. I felt awful."

He trails off, then he picks up my hand and starts bending my fingers gently back, and it's like the best touch in the world.

"I couldn't stand the thought of us finishing, Mel. I've been in this *state* – couldn't you see?"

I bring my other hand over and clamp it on top of his. We look like we're playing that kids' game where you pull out your hand from the bottom and slam it on the top.

"I dunno," I whisper. "I just thought you were fed up with me. I thought—"

"I was scared of losing you, you prat," he croaks. "I was *terrified*." And then he slumps his face forward and rests his forehead on our pile of hands. I laugh, pull out my hand from the bottom and stroke his hair, and I'm finding it hard to breathe. I've never felt this much before, not ever.

"I want to go back to how we were," I whisper. "I can't bear it if I've spoilt it."

"We can't pretend it never happened, Mel."

"No, but ... maybe we can get something good out of it."

He looks up, grinning, and puts on a jokey American accent. "What doesn't destroy us makes us stronger!"

"Yes. Yes, why not?"

"OK. Oh, this is brilliant. Look – from now on you gotta trust me."

"I will," I whisper. I can hardly speak.

"Finish your coffee. Let's go."

"Where?" I ask blissfully.

"Anywhere. Just wander about. Find a pub. Anything."

"Sounds perfect."

"But first ..." He picks up his phone.

"You got to cancel something?"

"No. I gotta send your friend a text."

He taps in some letters, smiling, and chucks his phone down in front of me. And I read:

```
Lisa - u gorgeous, plotting cow
- thanx 4ever!
```

Barrington Stoke would like to thank all its readers for commenting on the manuscript before publication and in particular:

Nicholas Banks
Mimi Batts
Kelly Belcher
Alina Bell
Amy Belton
Katie Brown
Nigel Brown
Laura Burley
Helen Coleman
Kieran Cox
Robert Crowther
Kelly Davis
Emma Dawes
Riu de Cavalho
Steven Dutton

Clara Flynn
Patrick Forsyth
Kirstie Foster
Petra Gregory
Rosemary Hicks
Jessica-Anne Hudson
Shelly Iles
Kathy Kainth
C. Karunanakaya
Abigail Lampitt
Kathryn-Louisa Lewin
Nicola Margand
Pamela Martin
Nicola McLoone
Joel McNamara

Clarissa Moncreiff
Stephanie Mullin
Abigail Nixon
Catherine Peters
Emma Richardson
Amy Rutland
Freda Sims
Vicki Smith
Daniella Turbin
Paul Watkins
Jacqueline Wilson
Roxanne Wishart
Hannah Wyatt

Become a Consultant!

Would you like to give us feedback on our titles before they are published? Contact us at the email address below – we'd love to hear from you!

info@barringtonstoke.co.uk
www.barringtonstoke.co.uk

Also by the same author...

Crow Girl

There's no light ... without the dark.

Lily is an outsider. Girls bully her, boys don't know she's alive. She begins to hide from her troubles at the nearby Wakeless Woods. But she is not alone. The crows are there. Watching. When she finds the crows, she finds herself – and a burning need to show everyone at school the *new* Lily.

Will this Halloween be a night to remember?

You can order **Crow Girl** directly from our website at **www.barringtonstoke.co.uk**

Also by the same author...

Crow Girl Returns

In the dark, the crows are rising ...

Lily used to be a nobody, until she made friends with the crows in the dark wood. Now Lily is Crow Girl. She's powerful and in love. She's somebody.

But that just makes the bullies want to hurt her even more. Lily has to end it. Once and for all.

Crow Girl is back. Watch the skies.

You can order *Crow Girl Returns* directly from our website at **www.barringtonstoke.co.uk**